Helen Orme taught for many years before giving up teaching to write full-time. At the last count she had written over 70 books.

She writes both fiction and non-fiction, but at present is concentrating on fiction for older readers.

Helen also runs writing workshops for children and courses for teachers in both primary and secondary schools.

How many have you read?

Two years on:

She's My Friend Now

 Helen Orme

Ransom

She's My Friend Now
by Helen Orme
Illustrated by Chris Askham

Published by Ransom Publishing Ltd.
Unit 7, Brocklands Farm, West Meon, Hampshire
GU32 1JN, UK
www.ransom.co.uk

ISBN   978 184167 740 8

First published in 2011
Reprinted 2012, 2014, 2015, 2016
Copyright © 2011 Ransom Publishing Ltd.

Illustrations copyright © 2011 Chris Askham

There is a reading comprehension quiz available for this book in the popular
Accelerated Reader® software system. For information about ATOS, Accelerated
Reader, quiz points and reading levels please visit www.renaissance.com.
Accelerated Reader, AR, the Accelerated Reader Logo, and ATOS are trademarks
of Renaissance Learning, Inc. and its subsidiaries, registered common law or
applied for in the U.S. and other countries. Used under license.

Meet the Sisters ...

Siti and her friends are really close. So close she calls them her Sisters. They've been mates for ever, and most of the time they are closer than her real family.

Siti is the leader – the one who always knows what to do – but Kelly, Lu, Donna and Rachel have their own lives to lead as well.

Still, there's no one you can talk to, no one you can rely on, like your best mates. Right?

6

1

Not fair!

'It's not fair,' moaned Kelly. 'Why is it just me?'

The Sisters were getting fed up with it. Kelly had been going on about it for the last two days.

They had just got back to school after the Christmas holiday. Mr Lester spoke to Kelly. She wasn't going to be in Miss Harper's maths group any more.

'But I don't like anyone in that group,' she said. 'And Sarah and Laura are there too.'

'But they aren't so bad if Kathryn's not around,' said Rachel. 'And she's in my group.'

'I'd rather still be in your group, even with Kathryn.'

The Sisters didn't like Kathryn. She was stuck up and she was always saying hurtful things to people. Her friends Sarah and Laura were nearly as bad.

'Yeah, but Mr Lester's O.K.' said Siti.

But they couldn't say anything to cheer her up.

It was their first maths lesson after break. They walked Kelly to her lesson.

They met up again at the end.

'How was it?' asked Siti.

'Boring! I didn't have anyone to talk to.'

'That might be a good thing,' said Donna. 'You talk too much!'

'Not any more I don't!'

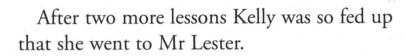

After two more lessons Kelly was so fed up that she went to Mr Lester.

'How can I get back into Miss Harper's group?' she asked.

'Work harder!'

'There's not much else I can do,' she told Lu later. 'I might as well work hard. Maths is no fun any more!'

'Was it ever?' said Lu.

2

Carly

Mr Lester wanted to talk to them.

'Can I go back to Miss Harper's group now?' asked Kelly.

'No!' said Mr Lester. 'Sorry Kelly, that's not going to happen.'.

Kelly pulled a face behind his back.

'But,' he said, 'I've got some news that might cheer you up. There's a new girl starting today. I want you five to look after her.'

'Why will that cheer me up?' said Kelly. She was in a sulk now.

'Because she's in my maths group,' explained Mr Lester. 'She'll be someone for you to talk to. You can stop fussing now.'

'What's her name?' asked Siti.

'Carly,' said Mr Lester. 'Come back here at break and meet her. Then you can take her to her lessons.'

Carly was waiting with Mr Lester when they got back to the form room.

'Carly, meet Kelly, Lu, Siti, Donna and Rachel.'

Carly looked at the Sisters. 'Hi,' she said.

'She doesn't look too happy,' whispered Rachel to Donna.

But Kelly gave her a big smile. She was looking forward to having a friend in maths.

Kelly took Carly off to her next maths lesson.

'Sit next to me,' she said.

Mr Lester looked at her. 'No talking,' he said.

'But Sir, I've got to show her what to do.'

'She'll do better listening to me,' he said. 'Now ...'

They were all quiet while Mr Lester was telling them what to do, but soon they had to get on by themselves.

Kelly and Carly started to chat.

Kelly thought she seemed nice. Carly asked lots of questions about Kelly and the school. But she didn't seem to want to tell Kelly much about herself.

3

Presents for Kelly

'At least Kelly's stopped moaning about maths now,' said Siti.

'What do you think of Carly?' asked Rachel.

'Not sure,' said Lu.

'She doesn't say much about herself,' said Donna. 'What has Kelly found out?'

'Nothing,' said Siti. 'But she's told Carly all about us.'

At first Carly had been friendly to the rest of the Sisters as well as to Kelly, but she was starting to act strangely. She was nice to them when Kelly was there. But if she met them without Kelly she often ignored them.

'She's just using Kelly,' said Siti. 'She's always asking Kelly to help her with her work.'

'Not just in maths either,' said Lu. 'She gets Kelly to help with other things too.'

Carly wanted Kelly to be her friend. She started bringing presents for Kelly. She brought bars of chocolate or other sweets. One time she even brought a bracelet.

Kelly didn't really want presents from her.

'It's just to say thanks for helping me,' said Carly.

Then Carly wanted to meet at the weekend.

'Can I come round to your house?' she asked. 'I'll bring a DVD.'

'I'm meeting the Sisters,' said Kelly. 'We're going to the movies. You can come if you want.'

4

She's lonely

The others weren't happy when Kelly told them.

'She's lonely,' said Kelly. 'She doesn't know anyone else.'

Of course, that made Siti feel sorry for Carly.

'O.K. She can come.' She turned to the others. 'Come on, give her a chance.'

The problem was that Carly just didn't fit into the group. They didn't have a good time.

'It was a bit much to 'forget' her purse,' said Donna.

'I'll pay for it all,' said Kelly 'It was my fault.' She felt really bad.

'She needs some other friends,' said Rachel. 'How can we fix it?'

'Maybe we can get Sarah and Laura to be friends,' suggested Lu.

'Not much hope,' said Kelly. 'You should hear them in maths.'

Then Siti had a really good idea.

'What about the drama club?' she said. 'We could all go, but maybe she'll find someone else to be friends with.'

Kelly told Carly about the drama club.

'Do you want to join?'

She was surprised when Carly seemed really keen. 'Let's go and do it now.'

They went to find Mrs Williams.

'Yes, we always want new people,' she said.

Carly was pleased. Until Kelly told her the others were joining too.

'Can't you do anything without them?' she said. 'I thought it was going to be just us.'

5

You don't need them any more

Carly was still a problem for the Sisters.

She kept saying nasty things about them. Just little things.

'Siti's so bossy, Lu thinks she's clever, Rachel talks too much, Donna shows off about her riding.'

Kelly was fed up, but if she said anything Carly looked as if she was going to cry.

'It's only that I like you so much,' she said. 'They don't deserve to be friends with you.

'And I haven't got any other friends. What will I do if you don't like me any more?'

'But I've been friends with them for years,' said Kelly. 'We've known each other since we were at infant school. Our mums always said we were just like sisters.'

'So that's why you call yourselves Sisters?' asked Carly. She went on, 'But you're grown up now. You don't need them any more. Be my friend instead.'

'I don't think this was a good idea,' Kelly told Siti. 'She's more clingy than ever.'

But they were all having fun in the drama club. Mrs Williams and Miss Giles were great.

'We want to do a play,' Mrs Williams told them. 'We are going to have auditions next week.'

Kelly and Lu got small parts. Rachel, Donna and Siti didn't get any.

'You can do scenery, costumes or make-up,' said Miss Giles. 'There's loads you can do.'

But the shock was Carly! She was brilliant. She was the best actor in the group. *And* she could sing.

'You're going to be a real star,' Miss Giles told her.

6

You were brilliant!

'You are brilliant after all,' Kelly told Siti.

They were all having fun getting ready for the play. So was Carly. She was much happier. Best of all, she had made some new friends.

Pete and Aziz were in the group. They both fancied Carly, but she said she was too busy with the play to go out with them.

'She's hardly spoken to me for weeks,' said Kelly. 'She doesn't even sit with me in maths any more. She sits with Pete now.'

'What are you going to do in maths then?' asked Donna.

'What Mr Lester said,' said Kelly sadly. 'Work hard and get put back up!'

It was the night of the play.

'You look fantastic, Carly,' said Siti. She and Rachel were helping Carly with her costume.

Carly was so happy she even smiled at Siti. 'Thanks,' she said.

'Is your mum coming?' Rachel asked.

Carly stopped smiling. 'None of your business,' she snapped and walked off.

'What was all that about?' asked Rachel.

Siti shrugged her shoulders. 'Dunno!'

It all went really well. Mrs Williams was very pleased with them. Carly had been brilliant. She was looking happy again.

Siti went into the hall to find her mum. Mrs Musa had brought Daudi to see the play. She'd left the little ones with the childminder.

'I'm glad to see Carly having so much fun,' she said. 'I didn't expect to see her here.'

'How do you know Carly?' asked Siti, in surprise.

'I worked with her,' said her mum. 'She's just moved into a foster home in our area.'

Siti's mum worked with children who had no parents to look after them.

Just then Carly came out. 'Hello Miss, did you come to see me?'

'That's Siti's mum,' said Pete.

'Yeah, I know. But she's my social worker,' Carly explained.

'You were great,' said Mrs Musa. 'Why didn't you tell anyone you were in the play?'

'I didn't know I could be good,' said Carly. 'But I might tell them next time.'

She linked arms with the boys. She looked at Siti.

'Good idea, drama club,' she said. 'See you next time.'